Life Under the Sea
Sea Slugs

by Mari Schuh

Ideas for Parents and Teachers

Bullfrog Books let children practice reading informational text at the earliest reading levels. Repetition, familiar words, and photo labels support early readers.

Before Reading

- Discuss the cover photo. What does it tell them?

- Look at the picture glossary together. Read and discuss the words.

Read the Book

- "Walk" through the book and look at the photos. Let the child ask questions. Point out the photo labels.

- Read the book to the child, or have him or her read independently.

After Reading

- Prompt the child to think more. Ask: Have you ever seen a slug on land? How do you think they are similar to sea slugs? How are they different?

Bullfrog Books are published by Jump!
5357 Penn Avenue South
Minneapolis, MN 55419
www.jumplibrary.com

Library of Congress Cataloging-in-Publication Data

Schuh, Mari C., 1975–author.
  Sea slugs / by Mari Schuh.
    Pages cm.—(Life under the sea)
  "Bullfrog Books are published by Jump!."
  Summary: "This photo-illustrated book for beginning readers describes the physical features and behaviors of sea slugs. Includes picture glossary and index."—Provided by publisher.
  Audience: 5–8.
  Audience: K to grade 3.
  Includes index.
  ISBN 978-1-62031-192-9 (hardcover: alk. paper) —
  ISBN 978-1-62496-279-0 (ebook)
1. Nudibranchia—Juvenile literature. [1. Sea slugs.]
I. Title. II. Series: Bullfrog books. Life under the sea.
QL430.4S39 2016
594.36—dc23
                                          2014041950

Editor: Jenny Fretland VanVoorst
Series Designer: Ellen Huber
Book Designer: Lindaanne Donohoe
Photo Researcher: Jenny Fretland VanVoorst

Photo Credits: All photos by Shutterstock except: Getty, cover; Thinkstock, 22.

Printed in the United States of America at Corporate Graphics in North Mankato, Minnesota.

For my husband, Joe—MS

Table of Contents

Under the Sea

A sea slug is hungry.

It looks for food.

Sea slugs crawl on the ocean floor.

How?

They move their flat foot.

foot

A sea slug
visits a reef.

It finds coral.

Time to eat!

11

Look!

This one finds a sponge.

Yum!

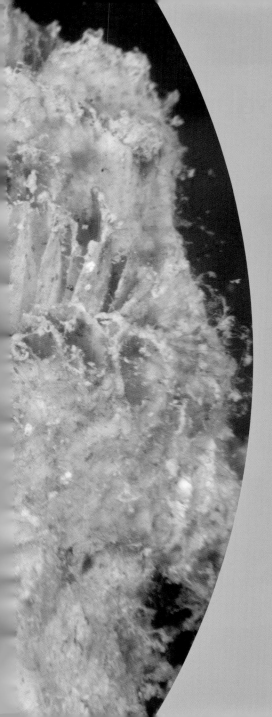

Sea slugs are soft.

They have no bones.

They have no shell.

Many sea slugs are bright.

Do you see its spots?

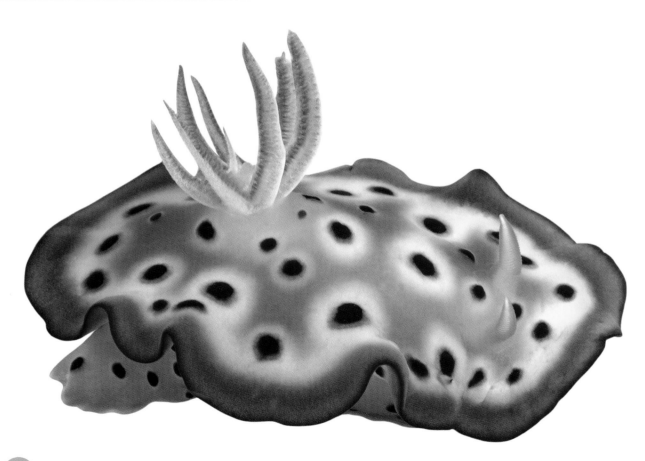

Do you see its stripes?

17

The colors say
stay away.

Sea slugs taste bad!

A sea slug hides.
It blends in
with the coral.
It is hard to see.
Can you find it?

Parts of a Sea Slug

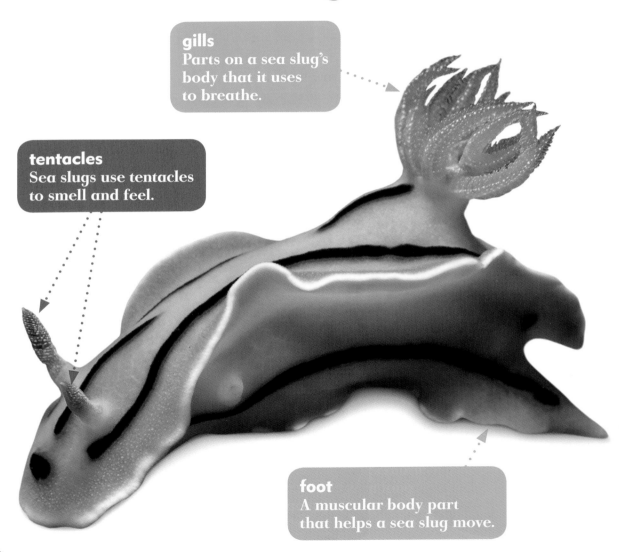

gills
Parts on a sea slug's body that it uses to breathe.

tentacles
Sea slugs use tentacles to smell and feel.

foot
A muscular body part that helps a sea slug move.

Picture Glossary

coral
Hard skeletons
of small
sea animals.

reef
A strip of coral
in shallow
ocean water.

ocean floor
The flat bottom
of the sea.

sponge
An ocean animal
with many small
holes that
take in water.

Index

To Learn More

Learning more is as easy as 1, 2, 3.

1) Go to www.factsurfer.com

2) Enter "seaslugs" into the search box.

3) Click the "Surf" button to see a list of websites.

With factsurfer.com, finding more information is just a click away.